W9-DCU-082

Real Reads

RR REAL READS

SENSE AND SENSIBILITY

JANE AUSTEN

Retold by Gill Tavner
Illustrated by Ann Kronheimer

Skyview Books

an imprint of

WINDMILL BOOKS

New York

Published in 2009 by Windmill Books, LLC
303 Park Avenue South, Suite # 1280, New York, NY 10010-3657

Adaptations to North American edition © 2009 Windmill Books

Author: Jane Austen
Retold by: Gill Tavner
Illustrator: Ann Kronheimer

Publisher Cataloging Data

Tavner, Gill
        Sense and sensibility / Jane Austen ; retold by Gill Tavner ;
illustrated by Ann Kronheimer.
            p. cm. – (Real reads)
Summary: In this retelling, the Dashwood sisters, sensible Elinor and
passionate Marianne, find their chances at marriage seemingly doomed by
their family's sudden loss of fortune.
        ISBN 978-1-60754-143-1 – ISBN 978-1-60754-144-8 (pbk.)
ISBN 978-1-60754-145-5 (6-pack)
            1. Inheritance and succession—Juvenile fiction
2. Social classes—Juvenile fiction   3. Young women—Juvenile fiction
4. Sisters—Juvenile fiction   5. England—Juvenile fiction   [1. Inheritance
and succession—Fiction   2. Social classes—Fiction 3. Sisters—Fiction
4. England—Fiction]   I. Austen, Jane, 1775-1817. Sense and sensibility
II. Kronheimer, Ann   III. Title   IV. Series
        [Fic]—dc22

Manufactured in the United States of America

CONTENTS

THE CHARACTERS

Elinor Dashwood

Elinor believes that emotions should be controlled. Will she be strong enough to hide her own heartache and offer the help her sister needs?

Marianne Dashwood

Marianne has a passion for life. Will her enthusiasm lead her into trouble? Upon whom should she rely?

Edward Ferrars

Gentle Edward longs to be a clergyman. Trapped by a promise made long ago, will he ever find happiness?

John Willoughby

Willoughby is handsome and passionate, and seems an ideal match for Marianne. But can she trust him?

Colonel Brandon

Colonel Brandon is middle-aged, wealthy, shy, and generous. Can such a man ever gain Marianne's love?

Lucy Steele

Why does Lucy seek Elinor's friendship? Should Elinor trust her as a friend, or fear her as a rival?

Sir John Middleton and Mrs. Jennings

Sir John and his mother-in-law are anxious to help Elinor and Marianne find happiness. Will their match-making succeed, or cause heartache?

5

Our cottage has been very

SENSE AND SENSIBILITY

Our cottage has been very quiet since my two older sisters left. Mama and I often sit together, discussing the events of the last two years. Oh, don't feel sorry for us. We spend half of our time visiting Elinor and Marianne, and even when we are here we are not short of invitations. Our neighbors, Sir John Middleton and his mother-in-law Mrs. Jennings, used to show very little interest in me, but now that my sisters are married they seem to have decided that, at the age of fifteen, I am old enough to be their next match-making project. You know how adults can be.

I must admit that I enter this bewildering adult world with some trepidation. After two years watching the confusion, intrigues, and intense emotions of my sisters' paths to true love, I cannot help but feel apprehensive about what the next few years might hold in store for me.

Two months ago, when all the heartbreak ended and my second happily married sister left home, I wasn't sure how to fill my time. Now, however, I have decided upon a project. I am going to write it all down, just as I saw it unfold.

When Father died, a complication in his will meant that he left all his money to our brother, depending on him to be generous to the rest of us. He wasn't. He moved his family into our beautiful old home at Norland, leaving us to find a modest cottage on a relative's estate in Devon. The day we left Norland, Marianne and I were in agonies of grief as we walked around the grounds.

"Oh, dear Norland; oh, happy house," wept Marianne. "Oh, dear trees." We pressed our cheeks against their trunks, the rain running down them mingling with our tears.

Elinor found us.

"Marianne, Margaret, we must control our emotions for Mama's sake."

"Oh, unfeeling Elinor," sighed Marianne, "you have not our strength of feeling, or you would not be so calm. And you have more reason than we do to be sad, as you will be so many miles from Edward."

A shadow momentarily clouded Elinor's face. "Marianne, you know that I greatly esteem Edward Ferrars, indeed I like him, but we really must exert ourselves."

"Esteem? Like? Oh, cold-hearted Elinor!" retorted Marianne as we all walked back towards the house. After some thought she added, "I suppose Edward lacks the qualities to inspire stronger feelings. He is kind and honorable, but his eyes lack fire; he lacks passion; he is tame and spiritless."

"You are unfair to him," replied Elinor.

When we reached the house, we discovered

that Edward had arrived to bid us farewell. "So," he said, looking sadly at Elinor, "you really are going to Devon. It is so far from here." Even though Marianne and I tactfully left them alone for ten minutes, Edward did not propose.

Later, in the coach, Elinor excused Edward's low spirits. "His mother wants him to be wealthy and important, but all Edward wants is a quiet life as a clergyman."

"Even so," said Marianne, "I believe that men ought to feel strongly, to show rapturous delight or deep despair. I shall be satisfied with nothing less in a man."

We settled surprisingly quickly into Barton Cottage. Our wealthy cousin, Sir John Middleton, occupied Barton Grange, a short walk away. "Such lovely girls," he beamed, "I'm sure you have left some broken hearts behind. Come for dinner next week. We will cheer you up. My wife is keen to meet you, and my mother-in-law will soon discover the secrets of your hearts."

With gratitude but little enthusiasm, we accepted his invitation. Without any real enjoyment, we met his cold wife and dutifully admired his young son. Elinor and Marianne endured his mother-in-law's teasing. "Now then, Margaret," laughed Mrs. Jennings, "your sisters deny having any favorite young men, but perhaps *you* can tell me the names of their beaux?"

Surprised to be spoken to, I looked at Elinor. "May I tell them?"

Everybody laughed. Elinor blushed.

"Margaret, you are just guessing," said Marianne.

"No I'm not, you told me!" I was enjoying the attention. "His initials are E. F."

Everybody laughed again, except for Sir John's friend, Colonel Brandon, who had hardly spoken all afternoon. "What do you think of the weather in Devon, Miss Dashwood?" he asked Elinor. A moment later, everyone's attention moved still further from me when Colonel Brandon invited Marianne to play the piano. He could not take his eyes off her as she entertained us all. I saw Mrs. Jennings looking meaningfully from Marianne to Colonel Brandon and back again.

The following morning dawned clear and beautiful. Marianne and I decided to explore the hills surrounding the cottage. Soon, however, the weather started to change.

"Oh Marianne," I said excitedly, "feel the wild wind in your hair."

She laughed. "See the angry gray clouds gathering, enjoy the cool rain on your face!"

"It's wonderful, Marianne, but I'm getting cold. Shall we run home?"

We ran down the steep hill with all possible speed. I saw Marianne slip, but I couldn't stop. When I eventually turned round, I saw a man bending to lift Marianne off the ground. He carried her straight down the hill and into our cottage without even knocking on the door. As he lowered Marianne into a chair, she was too embarrassed to meet his eye. Elinor and Mama thanked him. I stared at him. He was uncommonly handsome, with a masculine gracefulness. He introduced himself as

John Willoughby, the heir to the nearby
Allenham estate. "Please allow me the honor of
visiting tomorrow to inquire after your daughter,"
he asked Mama. Mama agreed enthusiastically.
I could see the glint in Marianne's eye as her
departing hero closed the door behind him.

As promised, Willoughby visited the next
morning. He and Marianne were soon talking
like old friends. Marianne discovered that
Willoughby shared her passionate taste in
music, books, and art. Their eyes sparkled with
enthusiasm as they read and sang together,
sharing their passion for life. When Willoughby
expressed his love of dancing, Marianne's face
glowed.

"He is just as a man should be," she told
us when he had left. "He is eager, with no
moderation, not at all like Edward or Colonel
Brandon."

Willoughby's visits became a daily event, and Marianne happily introduced him into our small circle of acquaintances at Barton. One day Elinor and I heard him teasing Marianne about the Colonel. "I do believe he rather likes you," he said provocatively.

"But he's thirty-five!" exclaimed Marianne in horror. "He's too old to be in love."

Willoughby laughed. "Did you hear him talking about rheumatism and flannel waistcoats? He is such a dull old bachelor."

Elinor looked disapproving and left the room.

That evening I heard Elinor talking to Marianne. "You are too open and forward in your affections. We know so very little of Willoughby. You must be more cautious."

Marianne disagreed. "I have been open and sincere. Would you prefer me to be reserved, spiritless, and dull?"

If she felt hurt by this comment, Elinor hid it well. "Your laughter at Colonel Brandon's expense leads me to question both Willoughby's character and your own judgment. Colonel Brandon is a sensitive, intelligent man who deserves our respect."

Marianne agreed to try to be kinder to the Colonel. Far from heeding Elinor's other warning, however, Marianne allowed Willoughby to show her around his home at Allenham, where her imagination needed little help in viewing it as her own future home. One morning, looking through a gap in our parlor door, I saw Willoughby cut off a lock of Marianne's hair, kiss it, and place it inside his notebook. When I told Elinor what I had seen, she told me off for not respecting their privacy.

Their devotion to each other was soon clear to us all. At dances and balls they danced with nobody but each other, and we all felt certain that they were engaged. However, even Elinor confessed to being confused that two such open natures should decide to keep their engagement a secret.

If we felt confused at that stage, it was nothing compared with our total bewilderment one morning when, just after Willoughby's arrival, Marianne ran hastily from the parlor in violent affliction. Without noticing us, she ran upstairs.

We entered the parlor to find Willoughby equally distressed. "I'm afraid I have to leave immediately for London," he told us.

"London?" repeated Mama. "I hope you will not be gone for long. You know that you

are always welcome to visit us here."

Looking uncomfortable, his eyes fixed firmly on the ground, Willoughby replied, "You are too kind, but I am afraid I have no plans to return."

We were too astonished to speak.

Willoughby turned toward the door. "I cannot discuss this further. It is folly to stay amongst friends whose company I can no longer enjoy. Please, always consider me with kindness."

We stared in amazement as his carriage sped him out of sight.

"Why did he not accept your invitation, Mama?" asked Elinor. "He is not a secretive person, but he is hiding something from us."

"Surely he has not been acting a part with Marianne," replied Mama. "Can we truly believe that he does not care for her?"

Elinor replied quietly, "He does love her, I am sure, but I want proof of their engagement."

Marianne walked into the room, her eyes red and swollen, and silenced our conversation.

Marianne would have considered her love for Willoughby too poor if she had been able to eat or sleep in the following days. She indulged herself in her grief, singing their favorite songs, reading their favorite books, walking their favorite walks. Elinor, who worried about her terribly, was relieved when Marianne finally agreed to join us on one of our strolls.

As we walked in silence, we saw in the distance a man approaching on horseback. Clutching Elinor's arm, Marianne whispered, "Oh, it is Willoughby," but as the figure approached we realized her mistake. Marianne's disappointment was somewhat relieved by her joy for Elinor, for at last Edward Ferrars had come to visit Barton.

Looking back, I remember Edward's surprising lack of warmth towards us. He hardly showed any pleasure, and confessed to having already been nearby, in Plymouth, for two weeks without visiting us. Poor Elinor must have noticed his coldness.

During Edward's week with us his mood improved slightly, but his behavior was inexplicable. At times he seemed to show his usual warmth towards Elinor, only to become suddenly reserved. When Marianne and I deliberately left them alone together one afternoon, Edward followed us out of the room.

Marianne, her passion heightened by her recent grief, accused Edward of being reserved. "Reserved?" he asked, reddening, "What secret can I be keeping from you?"

"Oh, I do not accuse you of any secret, but your character, your language are always so unnaturally calm."

"Maybe I am so foolishly shy that I seem negligent, but you and I also express ourselves so very differently. You want me to find these hills wild and rugged, I find them only steep and uneven." Elinor smiled as he continued, "You love crooked, twisted, blasted trees; I prefer them tall, straight, and healthy. A ruined, tattered cottage appeals to your imagination, whereas I prefer a snug farmhouse."

"So unlike Willoughby," sighed Marianne to herself. Then she suddenly exclaimed, "I never saw you wear a ring before, Edward! Is that a plait of your sister's hair within it?"

Glancing at Elinor, Edward turned a deeper red. "Yes, that's right, it is my sister's hair."

I looked at the ring. The hair, darker than his sister's, was exactly the color of Elinor's. She must have given it to him. They must have an understanding.

Elinor glanced at the ring too. I thought she looked pleased, but very surprised, to see her hair against Edward's finger. Surely he could not have taken it without her knowing.

Edward's departure confused us still further. He said he felt happier in our cottage than anywhere else, and that he had no pressing engagements and was not sure where he was going next. In spite of having neither reason nor desire, however, he left us. I noticed that he paid no particular attention to poor Elinor as he bade us farewell.

Marianne and I were disappointed by Elinor's calmness after Edward left. She kept herself busy and cheerful, neither seeking nor avoiding mention of his name. This could surely not be love. In contrast, Marianne left the room in tears every time Willoughby was mentioned.

Perhaps we were wrong to think Elinor was cold. Maybe she was just very self-contained. I did notice that when she was alone, she often seemed lost in sad thoughts.

The following week, the Middletons had a new guest. Lucy Steele, a cousin of theirs, was visiting from Plymouth, and they were eager to introduce us. At twenty-two years old, Lucy was beautiful, fashionable, and intelligent. Her conversation, however, soon revealed her limitations. "You must miss Norland terribly. Had you many beaux there? I always think they are so important."

Though we all felt that she was a little forward in her question, Mrs. Jennings was delighted. "Miss Marianne has made an excellent catch since arriving in Barton," she confided. Marianne's face paled. "His name is Willoughby, and we are sure they will marry soon."

"Mrs. Jennings, we are sure of no such thing," corrected Elinor, trying to spare Marianne more pain, but unfortunately drawing attention instead to herself.

"Ah, Elinor. We have discovered the owner

of the initials E. F." Sir John leaned over to Lucy, "His name is Edward Ferrars, but it is a great secret."

"Edward Ferrars!" exclaimed Lucy. "I know him well!" She stopped suddenly, then said, "That is to say, I've met him once or twice." Something in her face, deceitful and ill-natured, made me suspect that this was not the whole truth. But she refused to tell us anything further about her acquaintance with Edward.

Elinor was not keen to develop her relationship with Lucy, but unfortunately Lucy sought every opportunity to talk to Elinor. On one occasion I was reading, unnoticed in the corner of the room, when I overheard a conversation that changed my understanding of my sister forever.

"What do you know of Edward's mother, Mrs. Ferrars?" asked Lucy. "I understand that she wishes for her sons to marry into wealth."

"I have never met her," replied Elinor, "but I believe that you are right."

"You probably think my question inappropriate, but Mrs. Ferrars's nature is of some importance to me, as we are soon to be related."

"Are you to marry Edward's brother, Mr. Robert Ferrars?" asked Elinor.

Lucy fixed her eye on Elinor. "Not Robert Ferrars."

"Edward?" gasped Elinor. She looked at the nodding Lucy in disbelief. I feared that she was going to faint.

"It was always meant to be a great secret, but I'm sure Edward will not mind my telling you. He thinks of you as a sister, you know."

For a few moments Elinor was silent. I saw her struggle to compose herself before she managed to ask calmly, "Has your engagement been long-standing?"

"Four years."

"Four years?"

"We met in Plymouth. Has he not told you of his visits to Plymouth?"

Elinor must then have remembered, as did I, that Edward came to us from Plymouth the last time he visited. "Are you sure we are talking of the same Mr. Ferrars?" she asked.

"Yes, poor Edward, he suffers so much in our absence from each other. He recently begged for a lock of my hair, which he now wears in his ring. He says it helps him to feel that I am always with him." It was then that I noticed the similarity in the color of Elinor's and Lucy's hair.

Sobbing, Lucy talked about the obstacle Mrs. Ferrars posed to their future happiness. Uncharacteristically, Elinor did not attempt to comfort her.

"Do you think it would be better if we broke off our engagement?" asked Lucy over her damp handkerchief.

In vain I willed Elinor to say, "Break it off." Elinor remained silent.

"I hope I have not offended you by confiding in you," said Lucy, her sharp little eyes full of meaning. Elinor assured her that she was in no way discomforted.

Later that day I found Elinor crying. Realizing that I had overheard the conversation, she made me promise to keep Lucy's secret and to tell nobody else, not even Marianne. "Although I am suspicious of Lucy's reasons for confiding in me," she explained, "we would be wrong to betray her trust."

I listened to Elinor as she tried to think rationally about

Edward's situation. She felt that his engagement to Lucy must be the result of a youthful infatuation. Although confident of his love for her, Elinor knew that good, honorable Edward would not break off his engagement to Lucy. She wept tears for Edward rather than for herself. He could never be happy with such a wife.

Over the following weeks, nobody would have guessed that my admirable big sister's heart was broken into pieces. Anxious to spare Mama or Marianne any pain, she did everything she could to appear cheerful. Besides, how would she be able to explain her sadness without betraying Lucy? Nevertheless Elinor sometimes looked sad. Marianne however, absorbed in her own grief, failed to notice.

I was gradually learning that it is sometimes necessary to control our emotions for the sake of others.

In January, Mrs. Jennings invited Elinor, Marianne, and me to spend the rest of the winter with her in her London home. Marianne's eagerness to go to London, where she might see Willoughby, persuaded Elinor to accept the invitation.

After dinner on our first day in London, Marianne ran to her room. "I must write to Mama," she said. Later we saw an envelope addressed to Willoughby. Surely Marianne would only write directly to him if they were engaged. After her letter had been posted, Marianne frequently asked whether there had been any post for her, and spent hours sitting expectantly at the window.

One clear, cold afternoon, the sound of an approaching horse made Marianne leap from her window seat. "Oh Elinor, I do believe it is Willoughby!" She was to be disappointed again, however, when Mrs. Jennings opened the door to Colonel Brandon instead of Willoughby. Marianne ran upstairs weeping.

"Is your sister ill?" inquired Colonel Brandon.

"She is a little indisposed by the cold," explained Elinor. Anxious to change the subject, Elinor asked Colonel Brandon about London's weather.

Colonel Brandon visited daily. Although he spoke to Elinor, his eyes gazed at Marianne. His admiration for her was evident. Knowing Marianne's opinion of him, Elinor and I could not help but feel sympathy. Elinor's respect for him encouraged me to feel the same.

Three more days passed, and there was still no sign of Willoughby. An invitation to a party brought life back into Marianne's eyes. 'Perhaps he will be there,' she said excitedly.

Too young for a London party, I had to stay at home with Mrs. Jennings, desperate to know what was happening. The following morning I came downstairs early to find Marianne, half-dressed, writing a letter between bursts of grief.

I asked Elinor to explain. Willoughby had indeed been at the ball, and upon seeing him Marianne had leapt from her seat. Elinor had had to stop her from rushing to him. "Good heavens, Elinor, he is there!" Marianne had cried. "Oh, why doesn't he look at me?"

Elinor told me that Willoughby, who was with a beautiful young lady, was deliberately avoiding catching Marianne's eye. Eventually he was unable to avoid coming over to talk to them. He addressed them with cold politeness. "Goodness, Willoughby!" cried Marianne emotionally. "What is the meaning of this?

Have you not received my letters? Tell me, Willoughby, for heaven's sake, what is the matter?"

Looking very embarrassed, Willoughby bowed and turned hastily away, returning to the young lady's side. Marianne was so distressed that Elinor had had to bring her home immediately.

That afternoon a letter arrived for Marianne.
Elinor and I felt sick when we saw it. Following
Marianne to her room, we found her stretched
out on her bed, choked by grief.

"Oh Elinor," wept Marianne, holding out
the letter. "Willoughby is to be married in a few
weeks. He has long been engaged to another.
He says he has pleasant memories of our
friendship in Devon, and he is sorry if he ever
misled me."

Silent with disbelief, Elinor read the letter.

"He did love me, I know he did," cried
Marianne.

"But you were not engaged, were you?" asked Elinor.

"No. Oh Elinor, I am so miserable," cried Marianne, falling back onto her pillow.

"Marianne, for everybody's sake and to avoid further gossip, please control your emotions."

"Oh Elinor, how easy it is for you with no sorrow of your own. You cannot understand what I suffer. Leave me, forget me. How can anyone appear to be happy when they are so miserable?"

Only a sharp look from Elinor stopped me from saying what I really thought.

The following morning, when Colonel Brandon paid his usual visit, Marianne was too upset to come downstairs.

"Oh, not Colonel Brandon again!" she exclaimed.

Colonel Brandon was greatly concerned to hear that Marianne was unable to eat or sleep. Usually respectful of Elinor's silence about the affairs of Marianne's heart, he entreated her to tell him what had happened.

When Elinor had finished, Colonel Brandon looked awkwardly toward me. Taking the hint, I reluctantly went upstairs to see whether Marianne wanted anything. She didn't. When I returned downstairs, the door was open, but I didn't know whether to go back in or not. Colonel Brandon also seemed indecisive. I could see him sitting next to Elinor, "I do not know whether this will offer you any comfort ... " he said haltingly.

"If you have something to tell me that will help us to understand Willoughby's character," Elinor softly encouraged him, "then it would be the greatest service to us all for you to say it."

Should I leave? Should I knock and enter? Should I stay and wait until he had finished?

Feeling as awkward and indecisive as the Colonel himself, I found myself listening at the door.

The Colonel turned to Elinor, "You once asked me whether I was in London on business. I am not. I came to London to help the daughter of a dear friend. I have been responsible for Eliza since her parents' deaths fourteen years ago." He looked enquiringly at Elinor, wondering whether to continue.

"I found Eliza in great distress. Her innocence had been seduced, false promises made, a child born, and she completely abandoned and disgraced."

"Good heavens!" exclaimed Elinor. "Could it be – Willoughby?"

A few weeks passed. Having heard Colonel Brandon's story, Marianne treated him with greater civility. Although she felt some relief that she had escaped Eliza's fate, she still felt wretched. When news arrived that Willoughby had married the wealthy Miss Grey, Marianne realized he was lost to her forever. Even if this dissipated, selfish man had truly loved Marianne, he had always intended to marry for money rather than for love. He was not likely to be happy.

Feeling great distress for Marianne, Elinor ignored her own heartache and offered our sister devoted attention. She was sitting reading to Marianne one morning when Mrs. Jennings shrieked with joy, holding an opened letter. "Our dear Lucy is married to Mr. Ferrars!" she gasped. "Oh, how fortunate that you never formed an attachment, Elinor. Oh, how wonderful for Lucy!"

Excusing herself, Elinor left the room. Marianne and I followed her upstairs, where we found her sitting quietly at her dressing table. Marianne fell to her knees, weeping. "Elinor, this cannot be true!"

Elinor nodded. Clearly and simply, she told Marianne about her conversations with Lucy. Marianne listened in grief and horror. "You mean you have known for four months? During all my misery! And I reproached you for being happy! How have you coped?"

"By feeling that I was protecting you from further distress. Lucy told me about her engagement in confidence, but also in triumph. I had to listen to her boasting over and over again. Surely you can now see that I too have suffered and been very unhappy."

"Oh!" cried Marianne, "I hate myself! You, in your unhappiness, have been my only comfort. What gratitude did I show you?"

Even in her own distress, Elinor had to comfort Marianne. She explained her conviction that, although Edward's affection for Lucy had been replaced by love for herself, he had honored his engagement.

Marianne agreed. "Edward is the man most incapable of being selfish that I have ever known. He will always keep his word, even if it is against his interest and pleasure."

This praise of Edward's character made Elinor feel her loss still more deeply. That evening, as she and Marianne felt no

appetite for food, dinner was not served. This seemed rather unfair, as my appetite was unaffected. Elinor later told me that she was surprised by the pain this news of Edward was causing her. She thought she had prepared herself for it.

We had spent two months in London, during which time so much had changed. Now, Marianne was impatient to be home, and longed for the quietness of the countryside. Elinor, no less eager to leave London, planned our journey. We would break the long journey with a week with Mrs. Jennings's daughter in Cleveland. Colonel Brandon kindly offered to accompany us all.

Cleveland was a spacious house with extensive grounds. Upon our arrival, Marianne rejoiced with tears of pleasure. That evening, she enjoyed a walk through the long wet grass

of Cleveland's grounds. It was probably her foolishness in not changing out of her wet clothes that led to her having a dreadful cold the next day. What began as a cold soon developed into a fever, and by the third day Marianne's life was in danger.

Pale with concern, Colonel Brandon and Elinor discussed what to do. It was clear that Mama had to be sent for. Colonel Brandon offered to travel to Barton himself to ensure her comfort and safety. While the two of them spoke, their heads close together, Mrs. Jennings looked from Elinor to Colonel Brandon and back again. I too began to wonder. I could see her match-making mind hard at work again.

By the time Mama arrived the following morning, Marianne's danger had passed. Once reassured that her daughter would make a full, if slow, recovery, Mama turned her mind to other matters. "What an excellent gentleman Colonel Brandon is!" she exclaimed.

"What a noble mind! What openness! What sincerity! He has confided in me that he loves Marianne. I will do everything I can to help him gain her affection. Such a contrast with that Willoughby!" Poor Mrs. Jennings was most confused.

Soon after our return to Barton Cottage, during a visit from Colonel Brandon and Mrs. Jennings, we received a surprise visitor. We all looked in astonishment as Edward Ferrars, shy and awkward, walked into the room.

Although Elinor's breathing quickened, she politely invited him to join us. Edward took a seat with equal politeness.

This calm restraint was unbearable. "Why are you here? Is Mrs. Ferrars in Plymouth?" I asked impatiently. They all looked at me, and then at Edward.

"No, my mother is at home."

"I mean the *new* Mrs Ferrars," I said in exasperation. "Surely you know where your wife is."

Edward's face flushed as he slowly smiled, "Ah, you mean my brother's wife, Mrs. Robert Ferrars."

Now I too fell silent. Elinor's breathing was the only sound.

"You clearly have not heard," explained Edward. "Lucy Steele is indeed now Mrs. Ferrars. She married my brother Robert."

Elinor squeaked, ran from the room, and burst into tears. Edward followed her.

When we all sat down to a very pleasant afternoon tea only three hours after Edward's arrival, he had secured his lady, engaged Mama's consent, and declared himself the happiest of men. It took Elinor several more hours to feel truly calm. Marianne seemed satisfied with this degree of emotion. I felt quite dizzy. Mrs. Jennings was unusually quiet.

That evening, Edward's explanation of his freedom from Lucy met an attentive audience. As Elinor had suspected, he had been determined to keep his word to Lucy in spite of long ceasing to feel affection for her.

When news of their secret engagement had finally reached his mother's ears, she was furious. She immediately cut him out of her will, leaving him with nothing. She would now leave all her money to Edward's younger brother, Robert, who had always been her favorite. Being wealthy, he soon became Lucy's favorite too.

Soon afterwards, Lucy had sent a letter to Edward. "Robert has now gained my affections entirely," she wrote. "We cannot live without one another. We have just got married."

"This is the first letter I have ever received from Lucy which has given me pleasure," confessed Edward. "Her true nature is exposed, and I have had a fortunate escape. My mother will not disinherit Robert; her fondness for him will overcome her anger. Unfortunately, the news that Elinor and I are to marry will offer her no reason to reclaim me as a son."

With a fuller understanding of the qualities of both Elinor and Edward, I rejoiced at their wedding with all my heart. Colonel Brandon, who highly esteemed them both, offered Edward a living as a clergyman on his estate. Edward and Elinor were delighted. They now had their snug home and quiet, comfortable life. I cannot believe them entirely without design in their frequent invitations to Marianne to visit them on Colonel Brandon's estate.

Time and familiarity increased Marianne's respect for Colonel Brandon. Now, at the advanced age of nineteen, Marianne is discovering the falsehood of her own opinions. Unable to do anything by halves, she has grown to love passionately a man on the wrong side of thirty-five who occasionally wears a flannel waistcoat. With new happiness in his life, Colonel Brandon's spirits have lifted. Recently I saw them running together down the hill, the sound of their laughter reaching Elinor's cottage. I can't help thinking he's a little too old for such behavior, but perhaps I'm wrong.

Now they all live close together, a short journey away from Barton. As I said at the beginning, we spend a great deal of time there. We will be traveling again tomorrow. Before that, tonight, Sir John Middleton is throwing a party. He is eager to introduce me to a distant cousin of his. Mrs. Jennings is sure that I'll like him.

FOR FURTHER INFORMATION

The original work

This *Real Read* version of *Sense and Sensibility* is a retelling of Jane Austen's magnificent work. If you would like to read the full novel in all its original splendor, many complete editions are available, from bargain paperbacks to beautifully-bound hardbacks. You may well find a copy in your local used book store.

Filling in the spaces

The loss of so many of Jane Austen's original words is a sad but necessary part of the shortening process. We have had to make some difficult decisions, omitting subplots and details, some important, some less so, but all interesting. We have also, at times, taken the liberty of combining two events into one, or of giving a character words or actions that originally belong to another. The points below will fill in some of the gaps, but nothing can beat the original.

- Margaret does not narrate the original *Sense*

and Sensibility. She has a very minor role, is not confided in by her sisters, is rarely present, and does not accompany them to London.

● Their brother, John Dashwood, is married to Edward Ferrars's unpleasant sister.

● Jane Austen ensures that we understand that Elinor and Marianne have not been brought up to pursue men.

● Colonel Brandon's admiration for Marianne is evident early on. The reader respects him as a sensitive, sensible man. Among their new acquaintances, he is one of the few people Elinor really enjoys talking to.

● Colonel Brandon's story is more complicated than in the *Real Read* retelling. His true love was forced to marry his brother, but the marriage was unhappy. She had a child, Eliza, by another man. Before she died, Colonel Brandon promised to take care of the three-year-old Eliza. Marianne reminds him of his former love.

● At one point Colonel Brandon has to rush

to London. Everybody wonders why. We later learn that he had just had news of Eliza's relationship with Willoughby.

- Lucy Steele has an older sister, Ann. It is Ann, rather than Lucy, who frequently talks about "beaux." Lucy has enough sense and taste to correct her.

- After the ball in London, Willoughby sends a cold letter to Marianne. We later learn that it was his fiancée, Miss Grey, who dictated it.

- Edward's mother wants him to marry a wealthy lady called Miss Morton.

- While Lucy and Edward are still engaged, there is a very awkward meeting between Lucy, Elinor, and Edward. Jane Austen depicts the scene with wonderful humor.

- News of Edward's engagement reaches Marianne and Elinor before news of the marriage.

- When Colonel Brandon believes that

Edward will marry Lucy, he offers to help him.

- While Marianne is dangerously ill, Willoughby arrives. He explains his actions to Elinor. He did love Marianne, but still decided to marry for money. Although Elinor feels some sympathy, she still considers him a selfish man.

Background Information

Sense and Sensibility is one of Jane Austen's first novels, written when she was in her early twenties.

In Jane Austen's time, the relationship between marriage and money was very important. Women of her class were neither expected nor educated to work for a living. They therefore depended upon their family. Marrying a wealthy man was the most respectable way to gain independence and achieve comfort.

- The moral code governing relationships between men and women was very strict. This is why Marianne's open behavior with Willoughby is inappropriate without an engagement. Even writing him a letter is unacceptable. To have been too forward with him would have been seen as leading Marianne towards the same ruin as that faced by Eliza.

Jane Austen was writing at a time of major change. Revolutions in France and America demonstrated the potential destructiveness of new ways of thinking. Although Jane Austen does not include politics in her novels, we can see the influence of the ideas which surrounded her.

The period before Jane Austen's adulthood has become known as "the age of reason." Self-control was highly valued. In fashionable formal gardens even nature was tightly controlled. However, a new age, that of "feeling" or "sensibility," was just beginning. This new way of thinking valued freedom, passion, and wild landscapes. We can see that Elinor represents the importance of reason and control, and Marianne represents emotion. Although Elinor, like Marianne, experiences strong feelings, she has learned to control them.

We recommend the following books, Web sites, and films to gain a greater understanding of Jane Austen's England:

Books

- Enwright, Dominique. *The Wicked Wit of Jane Austen*. Michael O'Mara, 2007.

- Henderson, Lauren. *Jane Austen's Guide to Romance: The Regency Rules*. Headline, 2007.

- Hornby, Gill. *Who Was Jane Austen? The Girl with the Magic Pen*. Short Books, 2005.

- Le Faye, Deirdre. *Jane Austen: The World of Her Novels*. Frances Lincoln, 2003.

- Ross, Josephine. *Jane Austen's Guide to Good Manners: Compliments, Charades and Horrible Blunders*. Bloomsbury, 2006.

- Spence, Jon. *Becoming Jane Austen*. Hambledon Continuum, 2007.

Web Sites

To ensure the currency and safety of recommended Internet links, Windmill maintains and updates an online list of sites related to the subject of this book. To access this list of Web sites, please go to www.windmillbooks.com/weblinks and select this book's title.

Film

- *Sense and Sensibility,* directed by Ang Lee (Columbia Pictures Corp., 1995).

Food for thought

Here are some things to think about if you are reading *Sense and Sensibility* alone, or ideas for discussion if you are reading it with friends.

In retelling *Sense and Sensibility* we have tried to recreate, as accurately as possible, Jane Austen's original plot and characters. We have also tried to imitate aspects of her style. Remember, however, that this is not the original work; thinking about the points below, therefore, can help you begin to understand Jane Austen's craft. To move forward from here, turn to the full-length version of *Sense and Sensibility* and lose yourself in her wonderful portrayals of human nature.

Critical thinking questions

- Which character interests you the most? Why?

- Do you have more sympathy for Elinor or for Marianne? Why? Do your feelings change as you read the book?

- By which of her sisters do you think Margaret is more influenced? Does this change during the story?

- How do you feel about Lucy Steele? Why?

- Edward says that Marianne loves "crooked, twisted, blasted trees," whereas he prefers them "tall, straight, and healthy." How accurately do these images reflect their characters?

- Did it surprise you that Marianne could grow to love Colonel Brandon? Why?

Themes

What do you think Jane Austen is saying about the following themes in *Sense and Sensibility*?

- emotion and self-control
- honor and integrity
- love and marriage
- the importance of wealth

Style

Can you find paragraphs containing examples of the following?

- a person exposing his or her true character through words

- humor

- gentle irony, by which the writer makes the reader think one thing while saying something different; this is often a way of gently mocking one of the characters

Look closely at how these paragraphs are written. What do you notice? Can you write a paragraph in the same style?

For more great fiction and nonfiction, go to windmillbooks.com.